From Destroyed Webs To Masterpieces

Author
Pamela Elges Roesler

Illustrators –
Pamela Elges Roesler
Destyne Richardson

FROM DESTROYED WEBS TO MASTERPIECES

PAMELA ELGES ROESLER

Author:

Pamela Elges Roesler

Illustrators:

Pamela Elges Roesler

And

Destyne Richardson

ARPress
45 Dan Road Suite 5
Canton MA 02021

Hotline: 1(888) 821-0229
Fax: 1(508) 545-7580

Ordering Information:

Quantity sales. Special discounts are available on quantity purchases by corporations, associations, and others. For details, contact the publisher at the address above.

Printed in the United States of America.

ISBN-13:   Softcover   979-8-89356-176-0
                eBook   979-8-89356-177-7

Library of Congress Control Number: 2024914100

Mike was very unhappy.

The lady with the broom was always cleaning and destroying his webs!

One day, after a heavy rain,
Mike decided to climb down
from the ceiling.

4

Then he traveled
to the kitchen
and
scurried under
the
back door.

Everywhere he
looked, Mike saw
grass, trees,
bushes, and flowers.

What a beautiful sight
met his eyes!

"What an awesome place!" Mike said. "This is a perfect place to live."

He had his painter hat on,
a palette with paints
in one hand,
and a brush in the other.

He noticed birds hopping
onto tree branches
and decided those trees
were not very good
places to live.

He looked and looked
and looked.

Then he slowly turned around
and looked back at the
kitchen door that he had
just scurried under.

"I can build all kinds
of fancy webs
in that bush right
next to the door."

"Perfect. Just perfect,"
he said to himself.

He looked and saw that
the woman with
the broom was busy
cleaning inside her house.

"Now is the time," he said
and he scurried as fast
as he could go
to the bush.

He climbed up the bush
and found the perfect spot.
He spun a web.

Then Mike used his paints
to color and add
depth to his first
artistic web.

He spun a web displaying
pictures of his
brother, his sister,
and his mom.

He even did a portrait
of the
lady
with the
broom.

Just as Mike had finished
with the paintings, he heard
the back door open.

Out came the lady
with the broom.
She was sweeping and
had a serious
look on her face.

Her stern mouth changed
into a
very sweet smile.
"Oh my!" she exclaimed.

She came very close
to the bush
that had the artistic webs,
and where Mike,
the artistic spider,
was hiding.

Mike did not move,
but he was
ready to jump
to safety.

Then he noticed
a big smile
on the lady's face.

He heard her say,
"These webs
are amazing!"

"I need to
call my friends
so they can come
and see
all this fantastic
artwork."

"How amazing!"

And, her friends
did come from around
the neighborhood . . .
and from the city . . .
and from
far and wide.

Then it happened!

These friends called
their close friends, who
called other friends,
and they all came
to inspect
the fance webs
on the bush.

Everyone who saw
the webs
began to smile.

The day brightened.

And the lady with the broom
changed her everyday frown.

She began to sing and hum,
with a smile on her face.

"Well, what do you know,"
said Mike.
I can make a wonderful
difference
with my art."

What Mike did
not notice was
the smile on his face
as well.

The End